THIS BOOK BELONGS TO

EGMONT

We bring stories to life

Cover and interior illustrations by David O'Connell
Special thanks to Liz Bankes and Rebecca Lewis-Oakes

Text first published in Great Britain in 2019
by Egmont UK Limited
The Yellow Building, 1 Nicholas Road, London W11 4AN

Text copyright © 2019 Egmont UK Ltd
Illustrations copyright © 2019 David O'Connell

ISBN 978 1 4052 9478 2

www.egmont.co.uk

70476/002

A CIP catalogue record for this title is available from the British Library

Printed and bound in Great Britain by CPI Group

Stay safe online. Any website addresses listed in this book are correct
at the time of going to print. However, Egmont is not responsible
for content hosted by third parties. Please be aware that online content
can be subject to change and websites can contain content
that is unsuitable for children. We advise that all children are
supervised when using the internet.

Egmont takes its responsibility to the planet and its inhabitants very seriously.
We aim to use papers from well-managed forests run by responsible suppliers.

THE NAUGHTIEST UNICORN

PIP BIRD

ILLUSTRATED BY DAVID O'CONNELL

EGMONT

Contents

Chapter One: Magic Monday   1

Chapter Two: Through the Portal   16

Chapter Three: Unicorn Best Friend Forever!   29

Chapter Four: Dave's Doughnuts   53

Chapter Five: History Comes Alive . . .   65

Chapter Six: Perfect Prancing   74

Chapter Seven: An Unexpected Quest   93

Chapter Eight: The Fearsome Forest   107

Chapter Nine: To the Rescue!   118

Chapter Ten: Party Time   134

CHAPTER ONE
Magic Monday

It was Monday morning and Mira Desai was VERY excited. This was no ordinary Monday morning. This Monday morning was the first day of the holidays AND it was Mira's first day at a new school! Because this was no ordinary school . . . this was:

UNICORN SCHOOL!

Mira had been desperate to go to Unicorn School since her sister Rani started going two summers ago. Rani wouldn't stop going on about how wonderful her unicorn (Angelica) was. She kept saying how *amazing* she was at all the magical quests. And she was always making whinnying noises in Mira's ear to make her jealous. AND she'd brought home about a hundred Unicorn School quest medals, which had their own special shelf in the living room.

Rani said that quests could go on for days and days and were super exciting. And the time Rani spent at Unicorn School did seem like *ages* to Mira. But time passed differently at Unicorn School, and Rani was really only ever gone for a day in normal time.

Mira had dreamed of having her own unicorn since FOREVER. She practised plaiting the manes and tails of all her toy horses, persuaded her dad to let her groom his beard and even tried attaching a horn to their cat, Pickles. He wasn't very pleased.

It was a bit of a mystery who was selected to go to Unicorn School and who wasn't. Lots of people from Mira's family *had* gone to Unicorn School, including Mira's mum, so Mira hoped more than anything that she would get to go, too. Mira always tried to live her life as open to magic as possible. She wished on stars, she believed in fairies, she said hello to black cats who crossed her path. And then, one incredible day, Mira woke up with a sparkly envelope on her pillow.

Mira remembered it as if it was yesterday. (It was actually last Thursday.) She screamed so loudly that Pickles flung himself off Mira's bed into a pile of dirty clothes, and Mira's dad came running in to check what was wrong.

But there was nothing wrong. Everything was finally right. Her hands shaking with excitement, Mira opened the letter:

Dear Mira Desai,

We are delighted to invite you to join us at Unicorn School. You will be in Class RED.

Please use the Magic Portal to access the school.

We look forward to seeing you soon.

Yours sincerely,
Madame Shetland

'DAD!' Mira yelled and started jumping on the bed. 'I'M GOING TO UNICORN SCHOOL!'

Terrified, Pickles jumped on to Mira's dad's face and wouldn't let go of his beard. 'Mfmfmfmf!' he said cheerfully and gave Mira a thumbs up, before leaving the room and walking into the wall.

Mira reached inside the envelope and pulled out a leaflet containing all the information about the school, including a map and the School Rules. Mira thought she might faint with delight. Unicorn School was going to be BRILLIANT!

For one thing, Mira couldn't WAIT to bring home her own medals. She'd already started making a space for them on the shelf (and had *accidentally* knocked a couple of Rani's medals into Pickles's bowl).

But the thing Mira was MOST excited about was getting to meet her unicorn.

Her sister said that the unicorns were *specially* chosen for each person for specific magical reasons. You would get to spend all day every day with your unicorn: going to lessons, working on projects and going on quests. (Basically your unicorn would be your best friend.)

Mira did have a best friend already at normal school (Katie with a K) but she could definitely squeeze another one into her life. She'd spent a lot of time thinking about her dream unicorn best friend (Princess Delilah Sparklehoof). She'd filled a whole notebook with drawings of her and made a list of all the brilliant things they would do together.

UBFs 4 EVER

1. Have amazing, magical adventures!

2. Be great at quests

3. Get LOADS OF MEDALS

Before heading to the Magic Portal that would take them to Unicorn School, Mira's mum took them to the supermarket. Mira and Rani needed to get treats for their unicorns and Mum needed

to buy doughnuts for someone's birthday at work.

Mira was wondering what treats unicorns like.

MAGIC
BEANS

GLITTER
CLOUDS

RAINBOW
JUICE

Which aisle do you go to for magic treats?
she thought to herself. But when she asked her
sister Rani rolled her eyes and said, 'Unicorns like
carrots, *obviously*'. And so they all headed
over to the vegetable aisle.

When they'd bought their
carrots they went back to the

car. Rani also had some hay left over from last
term and Mum thought it would be nice if she
shared it with Mira.

The Magic Portal was in the car park by the
leisure centre. Mira had never actually seen it –
the portal could only be seen by current Unicorn
School pupils. Even Mira's mum couldn't see
it any more, since she had left Unicorn School

roughly a thousand years ago. Usually when they dropped her off, Rani got out round the corner so that she wouldn't be seen with them. But TODAY Mira would be going with her. And she would be one step closer to meeting her unicorn!

There had been quite a bit of traffic on the way and Mum was running late for work.

'It's okay, Mum,' said Rani. 'I'll take Mira through.'

Mum looked from one sister to the other and then at her watch.

'Fine,' she said. And then she fixed Rani with a LOOK. 'Make sure you take care of your little sister on her first day.'

Mum handed them their treat bags, gave them

both a hug and jumped back in the car. Rani had already started stomping off when Mum rolled down her window. She leaned out with her phone in hand.

'Girls! Let me take a picture. Your first day at Unicorn School together!'

Rani turned, tutted and folded her arms. 'MUM, are you crying? That's so embarrassing.'

Mum sniffed. 'It brings back such amazing memories of MY first day at Unicorn School! Oh, happy times . . .' Their mum stared off into the distance for a moment, before she smiled again and blew her nose. 'Now, smile girls!'

Rani rolled her eyes. Mira smiled and gave two thumbs up as Mum's phone camera **CLICKED**.

'Love you, girls. Have fun!' Mum drove off, waving one hand at them out of the window as she left the car park. Mira felt a bit nervous.

'Where's the Magic Portal?' she asked Rani.

'Over here,' said her sister. 'Come on.'

Rani stopped by the wheelie bins in the corner of the car park.

'So you have to get in the bin, spin round three times and then jump out and scream. Then you'll be at Unicorn School,' she said.

Mira looked up at the bin.

'Are you sure?' she said.

'Er, which one of us has a medal for being the Best at the Magic Portal?' said her sister.

'Okay . . .' said Mira.

Mira clambered into the bin and held her breath. This was SO exciting! (Also, it really stank.) In just a few seconds she'd be in Unicorn School . . .

UNICORN SCHOOL
THIS WAY

CHAPTER TWO
Through the Portal

Mira leaped out of the bin, yelling at the top of her voice.

'AAAARRRRRRGGGGGGH!' came the reply, as she collided with someone.

Mira looked down to see a boy on the ground, staring up at her with wide eyes. Behind him was a man cowering by a bike rack.

'Oh, hello!' said Mira, as she helped the boy up. 'Sorry about that.'

The boy stared at her warily.

'So this is Unicorn School,' she said, looking around.

To be honest, it didn't look very different to the leisure centre car park.

'Uh – no,' said the man by the bike racks. Mira supposed he must be the boy's dad because they looked quite alike and had matching briefcases. 'This is where you go through the Magic Portal to get to the school. Raheem is just about to go through.' He gestured at the boy, who gulped.

'But –' said Mira, as she looked around for her sister – who was nowhere to be seen.

And then she realized – Rani had tricked her and gone through on her own! TYPICAL.

'We can show you if you like?' said Raheem's dad. 'It's Raheem's first day. We've had twelve practice runs, just to be safe.' He squeezed Raheem's shoulder.

'Do . . . do you live in that bin?' squeaked Raheem.

'No! I was just . . . resting there before I went through the portal,' said Mira. 'It's my first day too – I'm Mira. It would be brilliant if you could show me.'

She followed the two of them past the bins and to a little clump of bushes at the edge of the car park.

Raheem and his dad showed her a gap in the branches where the air looked kind of wobbly and shimmery. Magic, thought Mira. Her tummy gave a little lurch. This was really it!

Mira waited for Raheem to say bye to his dad. It took a while because they checked Raheem's briefcase twice and then sang a song about the ten Rules of Keeping Safe. But finally Mira and Raheem crawled through the gap in the bushes and into a clearing. Everything looked just a little bit sparkly.

'Okay,' breathed Mira. 'Ready?'

'Erfg,' said Raheem.

Mira decided to take that as a yes. She grabbed his arm with one hand and reached out towards the sparkles . . .

There was a flash of light that split into the seven colours of the rainbow. Mira felt herself being lifted up and before she knew it they were hurtling through the air.

Mira's toes tingled and a giggly feeling tickled up her legs, into her tummy and arms and head. Even her hair felt excited. Everything was already so magical, she could hardly stand it. She was on her way to Unicorn School!

'HOW FUN IS THIS?' Mira yelled to Raheem, but he was too busy screaming to reply.

Just as quickly as it had appeared, the rainbow light vanished, and for a moment the two of them hung in the air, before dropping with a thump onto a soft haystack.

They climbed off the landing haystack, just as the next children were deposited by the rainbow. Mira looked around her and pulled strands of hay out of her hair. In front of them was Unicorn

School. It was HUGE. It had turrets and a clocktower and looked a bit like a castle, but lots of it was all on one level, like a bungalow. (Because unicorns don't like stairs, Mira thought. There was nothing about unicorns that she didn't know.) Rani had told Mira that the dormitories, where the pupils slept at night-time, were up in the turrets and that the unicorns slept in their stables.

The stables were in a large cobbled yard in front of the school. On the other side of the yard were fields with jumps set up. Those must be where the riding lessons are, Mira thought. She had never been horse-riding, but she had ridden a one-eared donkey at the beach last summer. She thought that unicorn-riding *must* be easier than that – and there would be less chance of falling in the sea.

Behind the school, Mira could see the forest and, behind that, enormous ice-capped mountains. Rani said that the Fearsome Forest was where lots of the quests took place. It was huge – stretching as far as Mira could see.

Mira's toes were still tingling. She turned to Raheem and grinned. He still looked a bit vomity from the journey.

The rainbow had dropped them off to the side of the Grand Paddock, which seemed to be the school playground for humans and unicorns. Real. Live. Actual. Unicorns! Groups of older kids stood chatting, each with a unicorn next to them, like it was no big deal. Mira realized her mouth was open in astonishment, and quickly closed it.

One group were playing football, but they were *riding* their unicorns, and the unicorns were kicking the ball with their hooves! And over in a far corner of the field some unicorns and their riders were leaping over the jumps. Mira thought they looked a bit like they were flying. Rani had told her that the unicorns developed magical powers as they got older, and that some of them could fly!

The excited feeling in Mira's chest got bigger and bigger until she felt like she might burst. The unicorns were all amazing – different colours with long legs, sleek, glossy manes and glittery horns. It was amazing to think that soon Mira would meet her very own unicorn!

Just then Mira heard a burst of laughter to her right. There was Rani and her friends. They were in the third year now – Class Yellow. You started in Class Red and then moved up through the colours of the rainbow. And each year you had another stripe added to your school badge. Mira looked at the badge on the sleeve of her T-shirt. What would it look like when she had a full rainbow?

'Um,' said Raheem, taking her out of her daydream. 'I think we go over there.'

Turning away from her sister, Mira followed Raheem over to a big banner near the stables that read:

WELCOME TO
UNICORN SCHOOL,
CLASS RED!

CHAPTER THREE
Unicorn Best Friend Forever!

The bell in the clocktower chimed and everyone gathered in their classes. Mira's class was the only one with just humans — each of the other six class groups were made up of children *and* unicorns!

Seven teachers filed out of the school. Each of them wore a different-coloured rosette with their name on. A tall, dark-haired teacher stopped in front of Mira's class. She was wearing a red rosette which said, 'Miss Glitterhorn'.

'Good morning, Class Red,' said Miss Glitterhorn.

'Good moooooorning, Miss Glitterhorn!' chorused Class Red.

'Now, before we head into assembly to meet the unicorns, I thought that it would be nice if we all got to know each other!' trilled Miss Glitterhorn.

Mira sighed. She was SO impatient to meet her new unicorn best friend . . . but she did like the idea of learning her classmates' names. After all, they would be her friends too!

A girl at the front put her hand up. She had blonde curly hair and was in a wheelchair with rainbow wheels.

'Yes?' Miss Glitterhorn beamed.

'Do you actually have a horn?'

'No, I don't,' said Miss Glitterhorn. She smiled.
'Now, we'll all play a getting-to-know-you game
where –' The girl put her hand up again. 'Yes?' said
Miss Glitterhorn.

'Do you have unicorns in your family?'

'No, I don't,' said Miss Glitterhorn. She smiled
again, although it was a bit smaller this time. 'So we –'

The girl put her hand up again. 'So, is it a coincidence that you are called Miss Glitterhorn?'

'YES,' said Miss Glitterhorn. 'Anyway –'

After seventeen questions Miss Glitterhorn decided that actually they would go straight to the assembly and they could get to know each other on the way.

Mira and Raheem walked alongside the girl who'd been asking all the questions. She told them her name was Darcy and that she was going to be famous one day.

'Wow,' said Raheem. 'How will you be famous?'

Darcy shrugged. 'I'll win a TV talent show probably.'

'My dad says those shows are for people with

no talent,' said a boy walking next to them. His footsteps were really loud and Mira saw that he was wearing cowboy boots. He had a mop of dirty blond hair and a smug mouth. Mira had heard him saying earlier how his parents were Olympic showjumpers and were making sure he was given the best unicorn.

Darcy opened her mouth to reply, but they'd reached the hall and a stern-looking teacher gave her a warning look.

Mira gasped when she saw the Great Hall, which was in the centre of the main school building. It was a beautiful indoor paddock and the grass was sprinkled with wildflowers. At one end was a platform, with a glittery

mounting block next to it. Around the sides of
the hall was a gallery for people to sit in. The
other six classes were already there with their
unicorns. Miss Glitterhorn pointed Class Red
to the front row. Mira felt a flutter of pride. Her
sister would be there to see her get her unicorn!

A hush descended on the hall, and a tiny woman walked across the paddock and onto the platform. Miss Glitterhorn joined her a moment later, clutching an armful of scrolls and a clipboard. The first woman introduced herself – she was Madame Shetland, the head teacher.

Madame Shetland cleared her throat and spoke into her microphone.

'Good morning children and unicorns, and welcome to a new term at Unicorn School. And an extra special welcome to our new students, Class Red, who I trust have been busy learning the School Rules in preparation,' said the head teacher. 'Unicorn School is a place of fun, magic and adventure – but it is something to be taken seriously. The bond between child and unicorn is a noble tradition, going back many centuries. Alongside your unicorn you will learn and grow – to undertake quests and become the protectors of our land, and shine a glittery light throughout the unicorn world.'

Mira felt a warm glow as she thought how she would definitely take it seriously. And she would definitely follow ALL the rules. As soon as she knew what they were.

The head teacher smiled at the gathered pupils. 'And, of course, even when not at Unicorn School you will take forth the lessons learned here and promote the principles of friendship, kindness, bravery and tolerance.'

After everyone applauded Madame Shetland, it was FINALLY time for the pairing of Class Red with their unicorns. Mira thought she might explode!

Miss Glitterhorn handed the head teacher the clipboard.

'Jake de Quincy,' said Madame Shetland, looking at the clipboard.

Mira saw a boy walking up to the platform. It was the one with blonde hair who was wearing cowboy boots. He was carrying his own riding hat with golden wings over the ears.

Madame Shetland held the microphone towards Jake. 'If you could tell us about yourself. Keep it brief.'

Jake leaned in to the microphone. 'I'm Jake. And I'm going to be a champion unicorn showjumper, just like my mum and dad.'

Miss Glitterhorn handed Jake a scroll, which he held up in front of him.

'The name of your unicorn will appear on the scroll,' declared Madame Shetland.

The class gasped as a projection of the scroll appeared on the wall behind him.

There was a hushed silence as they waited. The scroll shimmered and then a blurry word appeared. Everyone leaned forward to try and read it as the letters gradually became clear and sharp:

Jake and Pegasus

Then there was a loud noise from the front of the hall as the double doors swung open, making them all jump. Mira let out an excited squeal and Raheem nearly fell off his chair. Standing proudly in the doorway, was a sparkling, majestic unicorn.

He was deep purple with a dark blue mane and a glittering golden horn. He strode towards the mounting block where Jake waited with his arms folded and his eyebrows arched confidently.

Mira couldn't contain her excitement and gripped the hands of Raheem and Darcy, until Darcy muttered to her to 'get off' and Raheem looked really uncomfortable.

Jake and Pegasus walked away from the platform to the other end of the hall, and Mira felt slightly relieved that they wouldn't have to ride the unicorns in front of everyone.

Darcy was the next to be called. She wheeled up a ramp and onto the platform. Madame Shetland held the microphone towards her and Darcy grabbed it.

'Wow. What can I say? This moment means SO much. I want to thank my mum –'

'A speech is not necessary, Darcy!' interrupted

Madame Shetland.

Darcy's scroll appeared on the projection.

Darcy

and

Star

A dramatic whinny came from the double

doors and the class turned to look. A unicorn

came strutting in – her silver coat shimmered and

caught the light as she walked. She arrived next

to Darcy, swished her mane and struck a pose.

Darcy applauded in delight. They made their way

over to Jake and Pegasus, and started taking selfies

until a teacher confiscated Darcy's phone.

Next was Seb, who said he loved art.
He looked super-excited to meet his unicorn,
Firework, who had a rainbow-coloured mane.

Then it was Raheem's turn. He stayed frozen
to his seat when his name was called so Mira gave
him an encouraging shove to get him to his feet.

'Good luck!' she whispered. He gulped and made his way to the platform.

'My name is Raheem and I like books,' he said carefully into the microphone.

Raheem

and

* * *

I bet he gets a really clever unicorn, thought Mira. It'll probably be able to read and everything.

Raheem

and

Brave

A loud thundering sound could be heard from outside the hall and the floor seemed to shake. And then a blue shape came galloping into the hall. The unicorn was a blur, racing around the hall before coming to a sudden stop in front of the platform with a stamp of his front hoof. He was midnight blue and the biggest, tallest unicorn they'd seen so far.

Madame Shetland turned to Raheem, only to find he wasn't there, but she soon coaxed him out from behind the mounting block. Brave strutted over to the line of unicorns with Raheem following at a careful distance.

More and more children were called up. As each name was read out Mira felt her heart leap into her throat, and then sink back down again. Finally, she looked around and realized she was the only one in Class Red without a unicorn.

'And finally we have Mira Des –' began Madame Shetland and then she jumped to see Mira already standing next to her.

'I'm Mira. And I can't wait to meet my unicorn best friend,' said Mira into the microphone.

She looked over at her sister in the crowd, who gave a deliberate yawn. 'And I can't wait to win LOADS of medals,' said Mira. Madame Shetland looked at her and raised one eyebrow.

Miss Glitterhorn handed her the scroll. Mira's heart was hammering in her chest.

Mira

and

* * *

Everyone in the crowd turned towards the double doors. But there was no sign of her unicorn yet. Mira looked back down at her scroll.

She could see the word beginning to form.

It wasn't long enough to be Princess Delilah

Sparklehoof, but the first letter was a 'D' . . .

Dancer? Dasher? DESTINY?

Mira

and

Dave

A surprised sort of gasp echoed around the hall.

Mira peered closer at the scroll. It definitely said

Dave. Again the heads turned towards the door . . .

Again there was no unicorn.

Madame Shetland looked over at Miss

Glitterhorn, who said, 'Just a sec,' and jogged over

to the double doors. She started clicking and waving at something outside. But whatever was being clicked and waved at didn't seem to want to come in. Eventually Madame Shetland went over to help and between them they pushed in the smallest, plumpest unicorn Mira had ever seen. He had his bottom planted firmly on the ground and was making it as difficult as possible for the two teachers to move him.

Mira stared. He had a little pot belly and a mane like straw that stuck up at odd angles.

'Greet your unicorn, dear,' said Madame Shetland, giving a slightly forced smile. Miss Glitterhorn was leaning against the mounting block and sweating.

'Hi . . . Dave,' said Mira. The unicorn looked up at her. Okay, so he was a bit small. And he wasn't very glittery. But at least I have a unicorn! she thought.

Mira reached out to pat his nose and Dave snorted loudly and put his ears back. She pulled her hand away.

'A round of applause for our final pair, Mira and Dave!' said Madame Shetland.

Uncertain claps rippled around the hall. Mira's sister was laughing so hard that she had to be taken outside.

Mira looked back at her unicorn. There was a twinkle in Dave's eye. Mira felt encouraged. She smiled and waved at the crowd.

Dave snorted again and lifted his tail. Then he unleashed a giant heap of poo onto Miss Glitterhorn's feet.

CHAPTER FOUR
Dave's Doughnuts

It took Mira a while to get from assembly to her first lesson, as Dave had sat down again in the corridor and was refusing to move. But Raheem came to help her and together they half-dragged, half-pushed Dave down the hallway on his bottom and towards the classroom.

Unicorn School was certainly full of surprises. And challenges. Right now, Dave was being quite a challenge, but Mira was sure they would have a magical time as soon as they got to class.

Miss Glitterhorn tutted when they finally arrived. She was standing in front of the whiteboard, cleaning Dave's poo off her shoes with a wet wipe.

'As I was saying, Class Red, School Rule Number 19 is Be On Time, Every Time.'

Mira gasped. The double desks were like normal desks on one side, but on the other there was a taller, unicorn-sized desk with a bag of hay hanging off it. Underneath each unicorn's desk was a basket containing grooming equipment. Raheem scurried over to sit at the desk right at the front where Brave was standing proudly. There was one empty double desk. Dave plodded towards it, behind Mira, and gave a snort. Then he finished off his entire hay bag in two bites.

They'd made it! Mira gave a happy sigh as
she sat down at her desk.

Miss Glitterhorn finished running through the School Rules (Mira definitely heard at least some of them) and stood up from behind her desk. 'Now you have your unicorn,' she said, 'the lessons can begin. We will have two days of lessons, where you will learn all about Unicorn School, and how we look after the land. But, most importantly, you will bond with your unicorns so that on day three, you will be ready to go on your first magical quest.'

The class oohed and aahed, and there was a buzz of excitement. Mira looked around the room and noticed that Jake and Pegasus were their neighbours. She gave Jake a friendly smile but he was looking at Dave with a disgusted expression on his face. She turned and saw that Dave was gnawing at the corner of the desk. She hoped Miss Glitterhorn wouldn't notice.

'Right!' said Miss Glitterhorn. 'Lesson one is Getting to Know your Unicorn. You and your unicorn have a *very* special bond. You were chosen for each other by the purest kind of magic: friendship. But you've only just met and you must earn your unicorn's trust. First, grooming. This is very relaxing for unicorns. Pick up your brushes and off you go!'

Mira picked up a soft brush. She'd read all about grooming. She reached out to put the brush on Dave's back and he ducked, avoiding her hand, and side-stepped out of the way.

Mira stepped closer to him and tried again but he just did the same thing. Then she tried a different brush but he side-stepped again. They kept doing this and shuffling further and further away from their desk until a girl called Tamsin put her hand up to say that they were making her unicorn feel uncomfortable.

Mira dragged Dave back to their desk. She tried hiding the brush behind her back, she tried attaching it to a stick. She even tried brushing herself to show him how nice it was, until Miss

Glitterhorn came over to ask what she was doing. Then, hoping to put him in a better mood, Mira gave Dave the unicorn crown she'd made for him. Dave looked at the crown thoughtfully for a moment and then he ate it.

Mira suddenly had a brilliant idea. Dave must be hungry! That's why he wasn't paying attention!

Mira remembered Miss Glitterhorn saying Treating is Cheating (Unicorn School Rule 54) and You Must Not Bribe Your Unicorn (Unicorn School Rule 3), but this was tending to Dave's needs. She was looking after him! She reached into her bag for the treats she'd bought with Mum earlier.

But the shopping bag was full of doughnuts, not carrots! Mira realized she must have picked up her mum's bag by mistake ... now Dave didn't have ANY treats. (And mum had taken a bag of carrots to work with her.) Mira could feel her eyes welling up with tears as she dropped the doughnuts on the floor. NOTHING was going right today.

But something extraordinary was happening to Dave. His nostrils flared and his mouth twitched. With a happy little whinny he gobbled up a doughnut, then another and, before Mira could stop him, he had eaten them all AND the bag.

Suddenly, Dave was like a different unicorn. His eyes shone and his mane even looked swishy. He let Mira stroke his soft muzzle and then he stamped a hoof in joy. Mira grabbed a brush and started combing it through his mane. She looked around the room, fizzing with pride.

She hoped everyone would see how happy Dave suddenly was – he was showing his teeth in a sort of weird grin. He must really like doughnuts, she thought. Maybe she would win a medal for Best at Cheering Up Unicorns!

Then it all went wrong.

Dave reared up on his hind legs and let out
a loud and gleeful neigh. He shot forwards,
knocking over a chair. A few children and
unicorns turned towards them, startled, and
Miss Glitterhorn looked up from her desk.

Then, full of sugary, doughnutty
joy, Dave galloped around the
classroom, scattering the pupils and
their unicorns and destroying the
matchstick fairytale castle that Grace Hobbs
had brought in as a present for her unicorn and
had taken 'literally weeks to make'. Finally, he
skidded into Jake's desk and crushed his pencil
case. Jake looked furious.

After Miss Glitterhorn had wrangled Dave into

the Naughty Stall, she announced that since *most* pupils had successfully groomed their unicorns, the class would now be creating pieces of art together. She suggested that Mira use the time to read the rule book, paying special attention to Unicorn School Rule 79: No Havoc Indoors.

'That's one Havoc Point already, I'm afraid. Three Havoc Points will result in detention,' she said. 'Then, that pupil and their unicorn will not be able to attend the first quest.'

Mira felt a panicky feeling in her stomach. She couldn't miss out on the first quest!

ONE HAVOC POINT

She snuck a look at Dave over her shoulder and saw that he was happily snoozing in the Naughty Stall. He looked very sweet. But she couldn't quite ignore the thought she kept pushing to the back of her mind.

What if they didn't have a totally magical bond? What if Dave *wasn't* going to be her unicorn best friend?

CHAPTER FIVE
History Comes Alive...

After a good night's sleep in Red Dormitory, Mira woke up feeling full of hope for the day ahead. She picked Dave up from his stable and gave him a little pep talk on the way to class. At least he was walking alongside her today. Mira felt that was progress.

'I know it feels different, being in school now, like a big unicorn. But we'll get through it together! I know we can be best friends!'

Dave gave Mira a sideways glance and then did a long, rumbling fart.

The first lesson of the day was History of the Unicorn and their teacher, Mr Trotsky, was giving a lecture on famous unicorns of the last thousand years. Mira lost concentration a couple of times, first when another class rode their unicorns past the window and then when Darcy passed round a note saying 'Would you rather have a unicorn that could breathe fire or one that had electric hooves?' And Mr Trotsky did have a slow, droney voice.

'I hope you've been taking notes, class,' Mr Trotsky said, after talking for a very long time. 'We have another five hundred years of unicorns to get through after our break and then you will each prepare a presentation about a famous unicorn from history, to be performed at the

end of the day. Let's make history come alive!'

After break time Dave trotted over to the

grooming basket under their desk. With his front

hoof, he knocked everything out of the basket,

lay down in it and went to sleep.

Mira looked around at the other unicorns

who were sitting up nicely at their desks.

Some were even helping to take notes. Seb's

unicorn, Firework, seemed to be sketching with

his horn.

I'm sure Dave can do that too . . . when he's

awake, thought Mira. She smiled and picked out

different coloured pens to underline her notes.

That cheered her up even more.

Top Five Best Unicorns from History

- Unicornardo da Vinci – painter and inventor
- King Henry the Neighth – very fat unicorn who had six wives
- Winst-horn Churchill – unicorn prime minister during the war
- Queen Boudiccorn – the most magnificent Celtic warrior queen unicorn
- King Arth-horn and the Unicorns of the Round Stable

'Hey,' hissed Jake from beside her. 'Don't you know Unicorn School Rule Number 23?'

Mira shook her head.

Jake rolled his eyes. 'Unicorns Must Be Awake During Lessons,' he said. Pegasus widened his eyes, as if to demonstrate what being awake was.

Mira looked down at Dave, who was snoring. She nudged him with her foot and Dave let out a giant fart. Freya's unicorn, Princess, bolted out of the classroom in fright.

Mr Trotsky went to retrieve Princess and Mira felt a tap on her shoulder. It was Freya.

'Sorry I scared your unicorn away,' said Mira.

'Oh, don't worry,' said Freya. 'She's scared of everything. It's nice to have a break.'

'Well, at least your unicorn's awake,' said Mira.

'She's TOO awake!' laughed Freya. 'Here,' she said, handing Mira her sunglasses. 'Put these on him and then Mr Trotsky will never notice.'

They carefully put the sunglasses on Dave's head. Now you couldn't tell that he was asleep! Then, just to be sure, Freya got out her silver pen and drew eyes on the lenses.

Mr Trotsky returned with Princess. He glanced briefly at Dave before heading back to his desk. Mira breathed out in relief. They'd got away with it!

When it was time to do their presentations, Dave was STILL asleep. Luckily Darcy volunteered to go first. Darcy and her unicorn performed

a rap ('Darcy and Star, the best by far') and a
complicated interpretive dance based on Darcy's
favourite Disney film. Mr Trotsky said they did
very well to keep going for such a long time
but he couldn't give them a mark because it had
nothing to do with history.

Eventually it was time for Mira and Dave.
Dave was still asleep and was now gnashing
his teeth loudly (Mira thought he might be
sleep-eating). With some help from Raheem
and Freya, Mira dragged Dave's basket to the
front. Old Mr Trotsky peered at him suspiciously.

'I am here to tell you the story of a unicorn
that has, until now, remained hidden in history!'
declared Mira. She pointed at Dave. 'The Great

Dave-ius III. He was really good friends with Cleopatra and Jesus.' Mira looked over at Mr Trotsky, who was frowning. 'One day the Great Dave-ius III really annoyed a witch and she turned him to STONE!'

The class gasped.

Mira pointed at Dave again. 'He was frozen. He could not do anything except stare with his beautiful silver eyes. He was a statue for a hundred years.'

'What happened then?' piped up Flo, Freya's twin sister, from the front row.

'Um . . .' said Mira. The class looked expectantly at Dave. Who did nothing.

'And then he died. The end!' said Mira.

There was silence. Flo started clapping, but then she stopped.

Mira took a bow, but as she swept down she knocked the sunglasses and they tumbled off Dave's head and onto the floor.

'His EYES fell off!' shrieked Flo and she fainted.

'YOUR UNICORN IS ASLEEP!' bellowed Mr Trotsky, as Flo's unicorn, Snowflake, prodded her with a hoof. 'That,' said Mr Trotsky, 'is a Havoc Point.'

ONE
HAVOC POINT

ONE
HAVOC POINT

CHAPTER SIX
Perfect Prancing

'Maybe Dave's just tired after the lesson?' said Raheem at lunch as they ate their Rainbow Pie. (Rainbow Pie had seven different-coloured vegetables in it. Mira didn't think that was very magical.)

They all looked at Dave. After finishing his lunch in about three seconds, he'd gone back to sleep.

'Maybe he just doesn't like you?' said Darcy.

'What?!' Mira spat out her Rainbow Pie.

Darcy shrugged. 'Just saying. He's getting you in trouble a lot.'

'We can swap if you like?' said Freya. She hadn't been able to eat yet as Princess was hugging her so hard she couldn't move her arms. Raheem looked up. He was having a unicorn-free lunch as Brave had gone outside to charge around and leap over jumps.

'You can't swap your unicorn!' said Darcy, shocked.

Mira felt a bit sad. She didn't really feel she'd bonded with Dave yet. Mostly, he'd been asleep, grumpy or naughty. BUT he was who he was. And he was her unicorn!

Mira shook her head firmly. 'No,' she said. 'Dave *does* like me. He'll get the hang of school soon.'

'He'd better hurry up,' chimed in a voice. They looked up to see Jake standing by their table looking smug. 'If you want to go on the quest that is. You already have TWO Havoc Points and if you get three then that's detention and you have to stay here while we all go questing.'

'I wouldn't mind getting detention and staying here,' muttered Raheem as Jake and Pegasus strode away. Mira crossed her arms. There was NO WAY she was getting another Havoc Point and missing the quest!

ᴜᴜᴜ

Mira and Dave managed to keep out of trouble for the rest of the day. And the next morning it was time for their first riding lesson!

Miss Glitterhorn had said that the best rider would be given the honour of leading the quest. Jake had told them all that he'd been having riding lessons since he was a baby, so he was one hundred per cent sure he was going to be quest leader. Mira knew she wouldn't be the best, but she didn't mind about being particularly good at riding – just as long as she and Dave made it on to the quest.

Class Red filed into the meadow at the front of the school. It was being decorated for the first quest party. Glittery bunting hung from trees and hedges. Class Green were blowing up balloons and Class Indigo were helping Miss Ponytail, the Art teacher, set up a giant knitted scene of the Great Quest of 1488 (that was when Unicornardo da Vinci invented a horned helicopter and flew it over the Diamond Lake).

The first quest was a BIG deal at Unicorn School. When Class Red had completed their quest the entire school would come out to celebrate with them.

'What do you think the quest will be?' Flo was hopping from foot to foot with excitement. She was wearing a new homemade horn (she seemed to have quite a few).

'I reckon we'll have to climb a mountain and then probably fight a witch,' said Darcy, pointing at the glittery ice-capped mountains that loomed behind the forest.

Raheem looked alarmed.

Jake smirked. 'My dad said the first quest is always super dangerous and not everyone makes it back. Only the BEST unicorns and their riders.'

Raheem had to go and have a sit down.

Miss Glitterhorn rounded up Class Red by clapping her hands. 'It's time for your riding lesson, class! Please escort your unicorns to the stables to glitter-shoe their hooves.'

'Miss, Miss!' Darcy waved her hand in the air. 'What are glitter shoes?'

'Don't you know ANYTHING?' Jake scoffed. 'They're not glitter shoes, it's "glitter-shoe". Unicorns need glitter to protect their hooves before they can be ridden. There's a glitter-shoe box outside every stall.'

'Thank you, Jake, be nice, please,' said Miss Glitterhorn. 'Yes, glitter is *very* important for

unicorns. It keeps their hooves safe and makes
their horns sparkle. But the horn glitter is only for
very special occasions. Now, hurry up, everyone.
Glitter-shoe your friends!'

Once the unicorns all had glittered feet (and
Darcy had glitter-rimmed her wheels), they lined
up in the paddock. Miss Glitterhorn showed them
how to mount a unicorn using the mounting
block. Darcy had a whizzy harness which helped
her out of her chair and onto Star. Raheem
thought it looked a much safer way to get on
Brave, but Miss Glitterhorn wouldn't let him.

Dave stood very calmly next to the mounting
block while Mira put her hat on. That was a good
start, she thought. But then she tried getting onto

him and Dave kicked up his back legs
and tipped her into a bush.

Mira picked a clump of leaves out of her
hair. She stroked Dave's muzzle and gently
placed both hands on his back and climbed

onto . . . nothing as Dave trotted to the other side of the fence. Mira landed with a thump on the grass.

This. Was. Not. Fair!

The others were happily mounting and dismounting their unicorns and practising going from a walk to a trot around the edges of the paddock.

Mira could feel tears pricking at her eyes. Why didn't Dave let her ride? Why wouldn't he behave properly? WHY was he making Unicorn School so difficult? All Mira had ever wanted was to come here and make a unicorn best friend and earn loads of medals so she could put them on the shelf at home. Was that TOO MUCH

TO ASK?

Mira was really crying now. She put her hands over her face so that no one could see. She felt a nudge at her back.

Looking over her shoulder, she saw Dave. Mira sniffed. 'Leave me alone, Dave.'

But Dave ducked down and, with a flick of his nose, tipped Mira up and onto his back. Then he trotted over to the rest of the class and joined the back of the line, as the unicorns took turns weaving in and out of sparkly cones set all around the field.

Mira sniffed loudly and wiped her nose on the sleeve of her T-shirt. Then she leant down to give Dave a hug. 'Thank you,' she whispered.

Dave flicked his ears in response.

Over the next couple of hours they practised walking, trotting and cantering and communicating with their unicorns using their voice and their body. Dave didn't put a hoof wrong – and Mira couldn't stop grinning!

Then it was time to learn the unicorn and rider's most important skill: prancing. The unicorns had to pick their feet up high and bounce along. It was a bit like trotting and quite bumpy. Miss Glitterhorn shouted words of encouragement. 'Very good, Jake, but straighten your back. Not so bouncy, Flo! Raheem, just GET BACK on your unicorn . . . Excellent. Who's that? Mira! Mira?! Oh! Gosh! Well – excellent, well done. Lovely prancing!'

Mira was so surprised at getting praise from Miss Glitterhorn that she nearly fell off Dave!

Darcy grinned and held up her hand for a high five when Mira got back to the line. 'You guys are totally going to get a Best at Prancing medal!'

Mira couldn't quite believe it. For the first time, lessons were going well at Unicorn School. She stroked Dave's scratchy mane between his ears. He gave a proud fart.

Miss Glitterhorn clapped to get their attention again. 'I'm delighted to say that, for the loveliest prancing I've seen in a long time, our leaders for the first quest will be . . . Mira and Dave!'

Mira thought she might actually burst with pride.

'But . . .' Jake blurted out.

'Yes, Jake?' said Miss Glitterhorn, looking surprised.

'But my dad was quest leader on all the quests he ever did. He . . .' Jake's voice wavered and

88

he looked down and twiddled his fingers. Mira
thought he might be crying.

'Oh, Jake,' said Miss Glitterhorn, 'there will be
plenty of chances to be the leader. Now, one more
prance around the paddock then it's dinner time!'

The unicorns got into line but Jake was still
looking down and fiddling with something in
his pocket. Mira nudged Dave with her foot and
they rode over to Jake and Pegasus.

'Are you okay?' said Mira. And then she
stopped. 'Is that a doughnut? Why do you have –'

With a sly grin, Jake threw
the doughnut across the paddock.
Dave bolted after the snack,
which sailed over the fence.

89

Mira clung desperately onto Dave's mane.
Everything around her was a blur! Dave
soared over the fence and thudded down
on the other side.

Mira could see people and unicorns scattering and objects flying in all directions. Something was ahead of them . . . A colourful, glittering rectangular shape stretched across their path.

Then suddenly Dave skidded to a halt – Mira lurched forwards, but she clung on. She saw the doughnut lying on the ground just in front of them.

'Phew!' she panted, sitting up straight. Then Dave gave a buck and Mira was tipped out of the saddle. She went straight through the glittery shape and landed with a bump on the grass. She could hear voices saying strange things like 'The mural!' and 'I spent five years knitting that!'

'That – Mira Desai – is a Havoc Point,' said a very cross Miss Glitterhorn.

Mira stood up dizzily. 'But, wait . . . No! Three Havoc Points means . . .'

Miss Glitterhorn frowned. 'No quest for you.'

CHAPTER SEVEN
An Unexpected Quest

Mira sat in the classroom, looking at her drawing of Princess Delilah Sparklehorn. Everyone else had gone to the first quest farewell ceremony. She could hear them all cheering outside. Mira didn't want to go to the ceremony. She knew she'd feel even worse watching the rest of the class going off on their quest and seeing how excited they all were.

Jake had denied all knowledge of the doughnut and was made quest leader. The mural that Mira had sailed straight through, making a big hole, was currently being repaired by Class Yellow.

Mira sighed and put the Princess Delilah Sparklehorn picture in her bag. Then she set off for the PE office, where she'd been told to go for her detention. As she walked down the corridor she heard a snort and turned to see Dave trotting beside her. He nosed around in her bag.

'I don't have any snacks, Dave,' said Mira

Dave pulled out the Princess Delilah Sparklehorn picture.

'NO! Don't eat that!' Mira snatched the picture back and smoothed it down. 'Princess Delilah wouldn't have got me in trouble,' she said quietly.

Dave looked at Mira and blinked. Then he

carried on trotting down the corridor.

When they reached the office a fierce-looking PE teacher called Miss Hind was sitting behind a desk.

But she wasn't the only person in the room.

'Darcy!' exclaimed Mira. 'What are you doing here? Shouldn't you be on the quest?'

'TELL me about it,' cried Darcy. 'It's an absolute outrage! I have been making a VITAL contribution in every lesson.' Star snorted in support.

'Yes,' said Miss Hind, 'but you haven't done any of your work.'

Just then, in walked Raheem and Brave.

'What are YOU doing here?' said Mira and

Darcy together.

'I'm in detention,' he said.

Darcy frowned. '*Really*? What did you do?'

'I put a unicorn poo in Miss Glitterhorn's bag

and got three Havoc Points at once!' he replied, his eyes wide, almost as though he couldn't believe it himself.

'WHAT?!' said Darcy.

Unicorn poos were very small and neat and glittery, but they were still poos.

The teacher grunted from her desk and gestured for them to be quiet.

'Why would you get put in detention on purpose?' Mira whispered as Raheem sat down.

'I thought you might like some company!' Raheem grinned.

Mira wondered if it was more about not having to go on the quest but she didn't say that. Brave seemed quite cross with Raheem and was refusing to look at him.

'Did you hear what the task was?' said Darcy.

'No,' said Mira glumly.

'It's GLITTER-PICKING,' Darcy replied. 'It sounds absolutely *rubbish*. I'm *glad* we're not going.'

I'd happily go glitter-picking, thought Mira, as the teacher told them to stop talking again.

UUU

Miss Hind led them out into the stables. She pointed to a pile of dustpans and brushes and a poo shovel, and told them that their detention task would be mucking out ALL of the unicorn stables. Then she turned and headed into the PE office. They heard her turn on the TV.

'What?' said Raheem, horrified. 'I thought we'd be writing lines or tidying the stationery cupboard!'

'More poo for you, Raheem!' giggled Darcy. 'Well, have fun. Me and Star have stuff to do.' They scooted off to the other side of the stables, where they appeared to be looking at photos on Darcy's phone.

Mira wondered if you could get medals in detention. She hadn't imagined her first medal would be Best at Picking Up Poo, but at least it would BE a medal.

'Come on,' she said. 'We have a lot of poo to get through.'

It wasn't so bad at first – the neat little unicorn

poos were quite easy to pick up. But Dave's poos,
of course, were different. They were sloppy and
messy. And giant. Every time they cleared a stable
he would add a new poo on top of the straw,
like it was a fun game.

Mira paused for a moment and stared out
towards the forest. She wondered
what Class Red were doing now.

Then she saw a bolt of
glittery light shoot up from
the trees and into the sky.

'Guys!' she shouted.
'Quick!'

'What?' said Raheem nervously.

Darcy wheeled over. 'Hey, how's it going?
Oh, Raheem, you missed a bit.'

'They set off a flare!' said Mira. 'I read
about flares in the handbook.' She tried hard
to remember what it had said. She had been
distracted by the photos of the unicorns . . .

Then she remembered something Rani had told her. 'OH! It could be a DISTRESS FLARE! It's a signal that means they're in danger!'

Raheem's eyes went wide, but Darcy looked unsure. 'They're *glitter-picking*,' she said. 'The worst that could happen is someone could get trapped in a bin bag.'

'Actually they collect the glitter in special boxes,' said Raheem. 'And it's really valuable. And they said at the farewell ceremony that they need to collect loads to fill the Great Horn at the quest party, and they collect it at the Glitter Glade which is an amazingly special place. So glitter-picking is a *really* important que – ow!'

Darcy elbowed him and looked pointedly

at Mira. 'It's a *silly* quest and we are *not* missing out.'

Mira looked out one more time but the forest was still and silent. She sighed. The Glitter Glade sounded completely magical. She wished she was there now.

A few minutes later something made them all stop. A long, low howl rang out from the forest.

HhhhooOOwwwIIIIII

It got louder and louder, and then was accompanied by other sounds – screeches and rumbles. They all looked at each other.

'The Dangers of the Forest,' whispered

Raheem, fearfully.

'What?' frowned Mira.

'I read a book before I came here about all the possible dangers that lurk within the Fearsome Forest,' Raheem said. 'There were ninety-seven. And lots of them can be identified by their sound. That could have been a bear, or a werewolf, or an earthquake – an avalanche...'

More howling and moaning rang out from the forest.

'A land whale?' suggested Darcy.

'Should we go and get Miss Hind?' said Mira. She felt weirdly excited. Obviously she didn't want Class Red to be in danger, but if they were they would need rescuing . . .

'She might think we're being silly,' said Raheem.

Miss Hind *did* think they were being silly. She said the forest made all sorts of noises and that they'd probably imagined the flare. And she was very cross that they had interrupted her during a crucial moment in Champion WWUWF (World-Wide Unicorn Wrestling Federation).

'I'm *sure* something's wrong,' said Mira as they walked back out into the yard. 'What if they ARE in danger and we don't do anything at all?

We can't just stay here and do nothing!'

She paused for a moment and stared at Dave and then back at the forest. 'Team. I think it's time for a RESCUE QUEST!'

CHAPTER EIGHT
The Fearsome Forest

Darcy was very much up for the adventure and Raheem reluctantly agreed that they should make sure that everything was okay, as long as he could take some essential items with him on the trip. The items that Raheem considered essential were: *Dangers of the Forest* book, first aid kit, torch, sun cream, antibacterial hand gel, two changes of clothes, waterproof coat and trousers, high vis jacket, knee pads, notebook, special rock collection, lucky teddy, three packed lunches and an extra pair of emergency socks.

Brave was stamping his foot at the entrance to the stable yard, impatient for them to get going. He had stopped ignoring Raheem now that they were going on a quest and he was only a bit annoyed when he realized how heavy Raheem's rucksack was.

'RIGHT!' shouted Mira. 'We are going. On a QUEST. And we are going to rescue our class and we are going to get a medal for it. And we are going to have THE TIME OF OUR LIVES!'

Mira rustled some sweets until Dave woke up and then she jumped on his back.

'Okay people,' said Darcy. 'It's showtime. Which way are we going?'

Mira blinked hard and held out the map of the school grounds. Dave turned around and sniffed at it. 'Class Red were heading to the Glitter Glade. So, we . . . we take that path and follow it into the forest and then just as the path splits we –'

Dave ate the map.

MUUUNCcchHHHH

Raheem sighed. 'Well, now we don't have the map, we'd better stay here.'

'We don't need maps,' said Darcy. 'We'll follow our HEARTS! Or . . . just pick a random path and go for it.'

Star set off on the bridleway out of the school grounds. Raheem squealed as Brave galloped after them.

Mira gave Dave a pat on the neck. He did one last poo and then they set off after their friends.

∪∪∪

Everything seemed so much more bright and shiny to Mira as they rode to the edge of the paddock. This was a quest! An ACTUAL quest!

The entrance to the forest was shrouded in sparkly cobwebs and they began to pick their way carefully through them.

'Brave's stopped!' called Raheem, still outside the forest.

Mira turned Dave around. 'It's okay, Raheem,' she said. 'It's not that dark and terrifying in here, I promise!'

It took a while but Raheem and Brave *finally* came trotting through. 'It really was Brave, not me,' said Raheem crossly. 'He wouldn't move.'

As they made their way through the forest there was less birdsong and they could only just glimpse the sky through the thick branches up above them. Even though it was a bit spooky, Mira couldn't help but feel happy. She was on an actual QUEST (sort of) and Dave had been awake for ages!

'I wish we didn't have to trek through this terrifying forest,' muttered Raheem. He was struggling to stay on Brave who kept backing away from cobwebs and snorting wildly.

'I know what will distract us,' said Darcy, moving Star away from Brave, who was shaking his mane. 'Let's sing the school song!' She began to sing loudly and somewhat tunelessly:

'*We love our unicorns, yes we do!*

We keep them safe and glitter their shoes –'

Brave suddenly gave a strange, high-pitched whinny and Raheem pointed at the path ahead of them. It was blocked by three huge tree trunks.

'Oh no!' said Mira. 'I'm sure we're getting close to Class Red now.' She jumped off Dave and climbed up one of the tree trunks, brushing away more of the sparkly cobwebs. 'Yes! The path forks just up ahead, and the Glitter Glade should be down the hill on the left.'

'Let's jump it,' said Darcy, backing Star up to take a run-up.

Brave started shaking. 'I think he's trying to tell us something,' said Raheem.

'He probably just wants to go first,' said Mira. 'Brave by name, brave by nature!'

At that, Brave knelt down on the path and put his hooves over his eyes.

Raheem looked down at his

unicorn and then up at the tree trunks.
'Maybe he's scared of heights?' Brave
snorted indignantly and shook his
head.

'Look, Brave, me and Star will go first,'
said Darcy. 'You'll be fine!'

Star cantered up to the logs and jumped clean
over them. Darcy let out a happy whoop on the
other side.

Mira hopped back onto Dave and pointed him
towards the trunks.

'What do you think, Dave?'

Dave ran straight at the trunks . . . and then
scrambled through a gap at the bottom of
the trees, scaring away spiders and cobwebs,

with Mira clinging on to his back. It was a clever way to get through, Mira had to admit, even though she'd swallowed a cobweb or two.

Moments later Raheem and Brave came soaring over the trunks.

'It was the spiders!' said Raheem. 'As soon as Dave scared them away, Brave was fine!'

The unicorns and the children all high-fived each other, though Brave still looked a bit shaky.

'It's okay, boy.' Raheem patted his unicorn's neck. 'Spiders are harmless really. We got through it together!'

'Come on, Team Rescue Quest!' called Mira. She was still buzzing from getting past the tree trunks. NOTHING was going to stop them!

Well, until the unicorns' hooves slipped and
the friends found themselves tumbling down
a steep, muddy, leaf-covered hill . . .

CHAPTER NINE
To the Rescue!

Mira opened her eyes, rubbing her sore head.
She was at the bottom of a pile of Raheem,
Darcy and their three unicorns, at the foot of the
steep slope. Then a big shape loomed over them.
It said: 'YOU are supposed to be in detention.'

'Miss Glitterhorn!' said Mira. 'We found you!
We're here to rescue you!'

Their teacher helped Mira and the others
up. Mira could see that they were in the Glitter
Glade! It was a beautiful grassy clearing in the
trees, with streams of glitter running down

from the hills around. Everything sparkled. The unicorns were holding ornate-looking boxes in their teeth, which the pupils were filling with glitter from the sparkly piles on the glade floor.

But, Mira realized, no one seemed to be in any trouble. Everyone in Class Red looked ... well, fine. They were all staring at Mira and her friends, mid-glitter-scoop.

'Uh . . . we don't need rescuing?' said Jake, pulling a face at them.

'But . . . you sent up a glitter flare to ask for help.' Mira was suddenly unsure of herself.

'A what?' Miss Glitterhorn crossed her arms. 'Mira, that was a glitter *cannon* to celebrate the start of the quest.'

'But . . . we heard a moaning and wailing sound. We thought something terrible was after you!' Darcy was pulling leaves out of her hair from the fall.

Freya stepped forward and rolled her eyes. 'That was lunchtime. The unicorns wanted to sing karaoke.'

'That's enough, Freya, you know the unicorns

love to sing.' Miss Glitterhorn sighed.

As if on cue, Firework and Snowflake burst out into a howl, and then Princess joined in with several blood-curdling screams.

Mira winced. It sounded like the time she had accidentally sat on Pickles.

Miss Glitterhorn stared at Mira and her friends crossly. 'You are all in BIG trouble. We will deal with this when we get back to the school.'

Mira's heart was thumping. Could you get EXPELLED from Unicorn School?

Freya appeared at Mira's side. 'Don't worry. The quest hasn't been that fun. You didn't miss much.'

They looked over at Freya's sister Flo, who was rolling around in glitter with Snowflake and laughing with joy. Seb and his unicorn ran past with an armful of glitter shouting, 'THIS IS SO MUCH FUN!!'

'Well, it's a little bit fun,' admitted Freya.

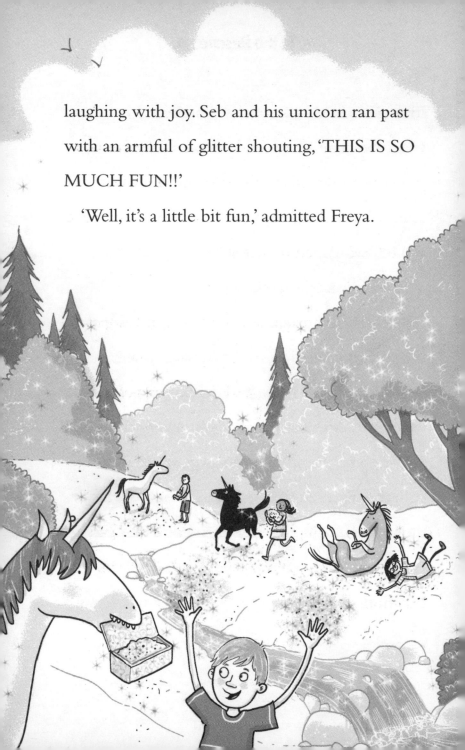

'But Jake's in a massive mood because Miss Glitterhorn said we couldn't collect the rainbow glitter from the edge of the Mystical Danger Cliff. It's too dangerous for First Years – you have to be Class Green or above.'

'Very sensible,' said Raheem.

Just then the glade darkened as clouds appeared in the sky.

Miss Glitterhorn clapped her hands and told the rest of the class to hurry up. 'Almost time to return to school, children! Remember, we must collect enough glitter to fill the Great Horn so the unicorns can glitter their horns at the party. And there is an extra medal for whoever collects the most glitter!'

And then the rain started. It was the suddenest, heaviest rainshower Mira had ever seen. The children were all soaked through within seconds. Darcy and Star and Raheem and Brave sped over to the nearest tree to shelter.

Mira was about to follow, when she heard a noise. She stopped, straining to listen over the rain. It sounded like someone calling for help . . .

Mira knew her teacher wouldn't believe her, not after the Rescue Quest turned out to be – well, neither a rescue *nor* a quest. And Miss Glitterhorn was busy gathering the class and the glitter together. Mira looked over at her friends sheltering under the tree. She couldn't risk getting them into even more trouble.

But what if she was right this time?

She looked around to check no one was watching her, gave Dave a nudge, and they both crept off down the path in the direction of the sound.

The path under their feet became more rocky. Then they saw a sign that said, MYSTICAL DANGER CLIFF UP AHEAD. Then another one that said, CLASS GREEN AND ABOVE ONLY PAST THIS POINT. Mira and Dave looked at each other.

'Shall we do it?' said Mira.

Dave trotted over to the sign and kicked it into a bush, and then looked back at Mira.

Well that was one way of dealing with it.

And then they saw it. An enormous cliff face,

covered in rainbow glitter. A narrow rocky path led across the side of the cliff to the edge, which jutted out over a ravine. There had been some sort of landslide, and the path was blocked by a huge mound of glitter. Standing against the cliff edge, on the other side of the mound, were Jake and Pegasus.

'Jake? JAKE!'

'Mira?'

Jake took a step along the narrow path towards her. A few glittery rocks crumbled off into the ravine below.

'Stop!' yelled Mira. 'Wait there, I'll go and get Miss Glitterhorn.'

'NO!' Jake backed up against the cliff. 'I . . . I don't want to get into trouble.'

Mira hesitated. Jake and Pegasus really were in danger on the cliff path, but she didn't want to get him in trouble with Miss Glitterhorn. And Mira was in enough trouble herself already . . . She made up her mind.

'Jake, we have to get back to school safely.

Just stay there and I'll go for help.'

But Dave wouldn't budge. He'd started eating the bottom of the rainbow glitter avalanche. Mira didn't even know that glitter was edible. But that had never stopped Dave before.

Mira nudged Dave with her knees. 'Dave, come on, we've got to get Miss Glitterhorn.'

Dave started chomping even more greedily. He was crushing pebbles in his teeth as he gobbled the glitter down. His bottom was wiggling as he moved forwards and he was making happy snorting noises. Dave and Mira were practically tunnelling into the avalanche now!

'What's happening?!' Jake sounded worried.

'We're just ... Dave's just ... eek!'

Dave took one last huge bite of glitter and

backed away. Mira gasped – there was now a clear

path to Jake and Pegasus!

'He's just . . . rescuing you!' Mira stroked Dave's ears and Dave gave a happy burp.

The rain stopped as suddenly as it had started. Jake and Pegasus tiptoed back down the cliff path.

'Are you okay?' asked Mira as Jake stepped off the dangerous path.

'Yes, I'm fine.' Jake still looked pretty pale and shaken.

'Why did you come to pick more glitter when the class were going back?'

Jake shrugged and looked down at his feet. 'Some of us have parents who actually expect them to be the best and not to mess absolutely everything up.'

Mira didn't know what to say to that, so they

trotted back up the path in silence. Except
for Dave's sparkly burps.

U U U

Mira and Jake caught up with their class on the
other side of the tree trunks.

'Where on earth have you been?' asked Miss
Glitterhorn as she was counting the pupils.

Mira looked at Jake, who had an expression
of panic on his face.

'Dave and Pegasus both needed really big poos,'
said Mira.

'Right. Thank you for the detail, Mira. Now
let's get back to school.'

Once they'd made it through the forest and
back to school, everyone hurried into the stables

to dry themselves and their unicorns off. The unicorns settled into their stables for a nap and a snack. Mira, Raheem and Darcy were told to write out 'I must not escape detention' one hundred times each before the quest party. The rest of Class Red all went back to change into dry clothes.

Mira could hear Jake boasting about how much glitter he'd collected as they made their way inside. She passed him in the corridor and Jake stopped talking and blushed.

'What was that about?' asked Darcy.

'Oh, I dunno,' said Mira. 'Come on, let's get ready for the party.'

CHAPTER TEN
Party Time

Mira was upset that she wouldn't be getting a medal in her very first quest ceremony. But she couldn't be too sad when the preparations were so much fun! The unicorns needed to be groomed and glitter-hooved and the pupils had to put their rainbow party T-shirts on.

That afternoon, Class Red filed out onto the paddock with their unicorns. The entire school was waiting and cheering for them. The knitted mural of the Great Quest of 1488 was back up and there was sparkly bunting everywhere.

Class Red all sat down in a row at the front. The school staff were sitting on a platform and there was something really tall and big hidden under a golden curtain.

Madame Shetland got up on the sparkly mounting block and clapped for silence.

'It is a very special day. Class Red have been on their first quest.'

The whole school cheered.

'They did a lot of glitter-picking and successfully filled the Great Horn!'

Madame Shetland nodded to Colin the Caretaker, who pulled the golden curtain away to reveal a giant, glittery, curved, upside-down unicorn horn. Everyone gasped!

'And I am thrilled to announce that the very special extra medal for Most Glitter Collected on Class Red's first quest goes to Flo. She picked seventeen boxes of glitter AND brought back another two boxes' worth in her hair and on her clothes. Such dedication to glitter-picking,' said Madame Shetland.

The entire school burst into applause. Flo skipped up to the stage to collect her medal, leaving a trail of glittery footprints on the way.

Madame Shetland clapped her hands again. 'Marvellous! Class Red, you may now come up to receive your medals for completing the first quest!'

Class Red all got up to collect their medals

from the stage. Freya, Tamsin and Seb all
whooped as they were presented with theirs.
Jake even did a bow. Mira, Raheem and Darcy
stayed in the audience, feeling a bit gloomy.
When Madame Shetland gestured to them to
come and collect their medals, Miss Glitterhorn
spoke loudly so that everyone could hear.

'Madame Shetland, these three pupils left
detention without permission to join the quest.
Therefore they will not be receiving any medals.'

Madame Shetland frowned. 'That is very
unfortunate. But the School Rules are clear:
Number 11 . . .'

'No Quest, No Medal,' said Mira sadly.

Just then, someone coughed from the stage.

Mira looked around to see where the cough had come from. Then, to her surprise, Jake started speaking.

'Miss,' he said, softly at first, 'they did escape detention –'

'All right, Jake, don't rub it in!' Darcy shouted at him.

'They did escape,' Jake repeated, speaking louder now, 'but it was only because they were worried about us. And actually, Mira saved me on the way back. I'd . . . got lost. They . . . they should get medals too. Maybe just small ones.'

Jake's cheeks were red and he was frowning and looking very uncomfortable.

Madame Shetland thought for a moment.

'This is very noble. But they did not complete the quest and they did leave detention without permission. That is *very* naughty.'

Darcy squeezed Mira's hand.

'However,' said Madame Shetland, 'their behaviour ultimately enabled them to help a fellow pupil. So, Mira, Raheem and Darcy, will you please come up to the stage to receive your medals for . . . Being Cautious and Concerned for One's Fellow Students.'

The whole school started clapping and cheering. Mira even thought she could hear Rani yelling her name in the crowd.

They gave each other high-fives as they got off the stage. 'Medals for being cautious, hey? Your dad will be so proud, Raheem!' said Darcy.

'He really will!' Raheem beamed.

'I'm sorry I got us into more trouble,' said Mira. 'But I had the best time with you guys.

Friendship really is the best kind of magic.'

And I *finally* got a medal, Mira thought as she stroked it happily.

The party was AMAZING. There were cupcakes and balloons and *glitter* everywhere.

There were dodgems, a bouncy castle and a coconut shy. And a long queue for the Glitter Horn. This was the highlight of the party for the unicorns, because it made their horns super-sparkly, which is what makes unicorns happiest.

Each pupil and their unicorn
stood under the upside-down
horn and when they were ready,
Miss Hind pulled a rope and
the horn released a shower
of glitter onto the pair.

Speaking of unicorns, Mira hadn't seen Dave since the Medal ceremony. She started looking for him in the crowd. Then there was a snort behind her.

'Dave! There you ar – oh!' Mira stopped, shocked.

Dave was wearing the chewed-up crown she had made for him. He'd put glitter in his mane and was wearing what looked like . . . gold mascara?

He was carrying a picture in his mouth. He'd dressed up as Princess Delilah Sparklehoof! Mira felt like she might cry with happiness. Then she laughed and gave Dave a massive hug. 'Oh, Dave! Did you sick up the crown and everything?'

He nodded. Mira gave him a kiss. 'Thank you.'

Mira led Dave to the cupcake table and held out the punchbowl for him to slurp. She looked around. She saw her new friends and their unicorns. She saw their quest medals and then looked at her own special medal. Nothing was quite as she'd expected at Unicorn School, but she wouldn't change a single thing.

Dave did a big poo next to the treats table.

Well, she might change one or *two* little things. Mira quickly dragged Dave away before anyone noticed.

'Come on, Dave, you need some more glitter.' Mira led him over to the Glitter Horn for their photo. 'You're not what I expected, Dave,' she said, 'but you're one special unicorn.'

As the glitter rained down on them,
Mira realized that she had had the best time.
And she couldn't wait to have more amazing
adventures with Dave the naughtiest unicorn!

WHO IS YOUR UNICORN BEST FRIEND FOREVER (UBFF)?

Answer these questions to find out who is your UBFF!

1. If you were having a unicorn sleepover, what would you and your unicorn BFF do all night?
    a. Sing karaoke, make up fabulous dance routines and take selfies.
    b. Go on a daring midnight adventure.
    c. Make friendship bracelets!
    d. Eat and sleep.

2. What would be your favourite lesson at Unicorn School?
    a. Drama. You like to be the star of the show!
    b. PE. You like to be super fit and ready for Quests.
    c. History. You love learning about amazing unicorns of the past.
    d. Lunch.

3. What makes you laugh the most?
    a. Surprises. BOO! Ha ha ha ha.
    b. Winning!
    c. You and your BFF giggle all day!
    d. Farts.

4. If you could have a superpower, what would it be?
    a. You'd rather be a celebrity!
    b. Flying, so you could SAVE people from DANGER.
    c. You would give super-hugs to make everyone you meet super happy.
    d. Invisibility, so you can sneakily eat as many doughnuts and treats as you want.

Answers: If you got ...

Mostly As: Just like STAR, you love the limelight and live your life to be as fabulous as possible.

Mostly Bs: You and BRAVE are made for each other. You're always up for a challenge!

Mostly Cs: It's hard to imagine anyone as loving and giving as PRINCESS, but that's you. You're kind and are always looking out for your friends.

Mostly Ds: Were you ever in any doubt? Your UBFF is DAVE. You're funny, friendly and completely true to yourself, no matter what the situation.

UNICORN JOKES

Knock knock
Who's there?
U
U who?
Unicorn!

Which unicorn smells?
The poonicorn

Which unicorn has carriages and runs on steam?
The choo-choo-nicorn

What is a unicorn's favourite type of story?
Fairy tails

What do you call a unicorn without a horn?
Pointless

Where do sick unicorns go?
The horsepital

What's a unicorn's favourite hair style?
Pony tail

Look out for more brilliant
adventures with Dave and Mira!

The Naughtiest Unicorn at Sports Day

The Naughtiest Unicorn and the School Disco

The Naughtiest Unicorn at Christmas